ADVENTURES OF RAGGEDY ANN

ADVENTURES OF RAGGEDY ANN

WRITTEN AND
ILLUSTRATED BY

JOHNNY GRUELLE

This edition is distributed by
AVENEL BOOKS
a division of Crown Publishers, Inc.

PREFACE AND DEDICATION

As I write this, I have before me on my desk, propped up against the telephone, an old rag doll. Dear old Raggedy Ann!

The same Raggedy Ann with which my mother played when a child.

There she sits, a trifle loppy and loose-jointed, looking me squarely in the face in a straightforward, honest manner, a twinkle where her shoe-button eyes reflect the light.

Evidently Raggedy has been to a "tea party" today, for her face is covered with chocolate.

She smiles happily and continuously.

True, she has been nibbled by mice, who have made nests out of the soft cotton with which she has been stuffed, but Raggedy smiled just as broadly when the mice nibbled at her, for her smile is painted on.

What adventures you must have had, Raggedy!

What joy and happiness you have brought into this world!

And no matter what treatment you have received, how patient you have been!

What lessons of kindness and fortitude you might teach could you but talk; you with your wisdom of fifty-nine years. No wonder Rag Dolls are the best beloved! You are so kindly, so patient, so lovable.

The more you become torn, tattered and loose-jointed, Rag Dolls, the more you are loved by children.

Who knows but that Fairyland is filled with old, lovable

Rag Dolls—soft, loppy Rag Dolls who ride through all the wonders of Fairyland in the crook of dimpled arms, snuggling close to childish breasts within which beat hearts filled with eternal sunshine.

So, to the millions of children and grown-ups who have loved a Rag Doll, I dedicate these stories of Raggedy Ann.

JOHNNY GRUELLE.

INTRODUCTION

MARCELLA liked to play up in the attic at Grandma's quaint old house, 'way out in the country, for there were so many old forgotten things to find up there.

One day when Marcella was up in the attic and had played with the old spinning wheel until she had grown tired of it, she curled up on an old horse-hair sofa to rest.

"I wonder what is in that barrel, 'way back in the corner?" she thought, as she jumped from the sofa and climbed over two dusty trunks to the barrel standing back under the eaves.

It was quite dark back there, so when Marcella had pulled a large bundle of things from the barrel she took them over to the dormer window where she could see better. There was a funny little bonnet with long white ribbons. Marcella put it on.

In an old leather bag she found a number of tin-types of queer looking men and women in old-fashioned clothes. And there was one picture of a very pretty little girl with long curls tied tightly back from her forehead and wearing a long dress and queer pantaloons which reached to her shoe-tops. And then out of the heap she pulled an old rag doll with only one shoe-button eye and a painted nose and a smiling mouth. Her dress was of soft material, blue with pretty little flowers and dots all over it.

Forgetting everything else in the happiness of her find, Marcella caught up the rag doll and ran downstairs to show it to Grandma.

"Well! Well! Where did you find it?" Grandma cried. "It's old Raggedy Ann!" she went on as she hugged the doll to her breast. "I had forgotten her. She has been in the attic for fifty years, I guess! Well! Well! Dear old Raggedy Ann! I will sew another button on her right away!" and Grandma went to the machine drawer and got her needle and thread.

Marcella watched the sewing while Grandma told how she had played with Raggedy Ann when she was a little girl.

"Now!" Grandma laughed, "Raggedy Ann, you have two fine shoe-button eyes and with them you can see the changes that have taken place in the world while you have been shut up so long in the attic! For, Raggedy Ann, you have a new playmate and mistress now, and I hope you both will have as much happiness together as you and I used to have!"

Then Grandma gave Raggedy Ann to Marcella, saying very seriously, "Marcella, let me introduce my very dear friend, Raggedy Ann. Raggedy, this is my granddaughter, Marcella!" And Grandma gave the doll a twitch with her fingers in such a way that the rag doll nodded her head to Marcella.

"Oh, Grandma! Thank you ever and ever so much!" Marcella cried as she gave Grandma a hug and kiss. "Raggedy Ann and I will have just loads of fun."

And this is how Raggedy Ann joined the doll family at Marcella's house, where she began the adventures of Raggedy Ann, told in the following stories.

CONTENTS

RAGGEDY ANN LEARNS A LESSON

RAGGEDY ANN LEARNS A LESSON

ONE day the dolls were left all to themselves.

Their little mistress had placed them all around the room and told them to be nice children while she was away.

And there they sat and never even so much as wiggled a finger, until their mistress had left the room.

Then the soldier dolly turned his head and solemnly winked at Raggedy Ann.

And when the front gate clicked and the dollies knew they were alone, they all scrambled to their feet.

"Now let's have a good time!" cried the tin soldier. "Let's all go in search of something to eat!"

"Yes! Let's all go in search of something to eat!" cried all the other dollies.

"When Mistress had me out playing with me this morning," said Raggedy Ann, "she carried me by a door near the back of the house and I smelled something which smelled as if it would taste delicious!"

"Then you lead the way, Raggedy Ann!" cried the French dolly.

"I think it would be a good plan to elect Raggedy Ann as our leader on this expedition!" said the Indian doll.

At this all the other dolls clapped their hands together and shouted, "Hurrah! Raggedy Ann will be our leader."

So Raggedy Ann, very proud indeed to have the confidence and love of all the other dollies, said that she would be very glad to be their leader.

"Follow me!" she cried as her wobbly legs carried her across the floor at a lively pace.

The other dollies followed, racing about the house until they came to the pantry door. "This is the place!" cried Raggedy Ann, and sure enough, all the dollies smelled something which they knew must be very good to eat.

But none of the dollies was tall enough to open the door and, although they pushed and pulled with all their might, the door remained tightly closed.

The dollies were talking and pulling and pushing and every once in a while one would fall over and the others would step on her in their efforts to open the door. Finally Raggedy Ann drew away and sat down on the floor.

When the other dollies discovered Raggedy Ann sitting there, running her rag hands through her yarn hair, they knew she was thinking.

"Sh! Sh!" they said to each other and quietly went over near Raggedy Ann and sat down in front of her.

"There must be a way!" said Raggedy Ann.

"Raggedy says there must be a way to get inside!" cried

all the dolls.

"I can't seem to think clearly to-day," said Raggedy Ann. "It feels as if my head were ripped."

At this the French doll ran to Raggedy Ann and took off her bonnet. "Yes, there is a rip in your head, Raggedy!" she said and she pulled a pin from her skirt and pinned up Raggedy's head. "It's not a very neat job, for I got some puckers in it!" she said.

"Oh that is ever so much better!" cried Raggedy Ann. "Now I can think quite clearly."

"Now Raggedy can think clearly!" cried all the dolls.

"My thoughts must have leaked out the rip before!" said Raggedy Ann.

"They must have leaked out before, dear Raggedy!" cried all the other dolls.

"Now that I can think so clearly," said Raggedy Ann, "I think the door must be locked and to get in we must unlock it!"

"That will be easy!" said the Dutch doll who says "Mamma" when he is tipped backward and forward, "For the brave tin soldier can shoot the key out of the lock!"

"I can easily do that!" cried the tin soldier, as he raised his gun.

"Oh, Raggedy Ann!" cried the French dolly, "Please do not let him shoot!"

"No!" said Raggedy Ann, "We must think of a quieter way!"

After thinking quite hard for a moment, Raggedy Ann jumped up and said: "I have it!" And she caught up the Jumping Jack and held him up to the door; then Jack slid up his stick and unlocked the door.

Then the dollies all pushed and the door swung open.

My! Such a scramble! The dolls piled over one another in their desire to be the first at the goodies.

They swarmed upon the pantry shelves and in their eagerness spilled a pitcher of cream which ran all over the French dolly's dress.

The Indian doll found some corn bread and dipping it in the molasses he sat down for a good feast.

A jar of raspberry jam was overturned and the dollies ate of this until their faces were all purple.

The tin soldier fell from the shelf three times and bent one of his tin legs, but he scrambled right back up again.

Never had the dolls had so much fun and excitement, and they had all eaten their fill when they heard the click of the front gate.

They did not take time to climb from the shelves, but all rolled or jumped off to the floor and scrambled back to their room as fast as they could run, leaving a trail of bread crumbs and jam along the way back to the nursery.

Just as their mistress came into the room the dolls dropped in whatever positions they happened to be in.

"This is funny!" cried Mistress. "They were all left sitting in their places around the room! I wonder if Fido has been shaking them up!" Then she saw Raggedy Ann's face and picked her up. "Why Raggedy Ann, you are all sticky! I do believe you are covered with jam!" and Mistress tasted

Raggedy Ann's hand. "Yes! It's JAM! Shame on you Raggedy Ann! You've been in the pantry and all the others, too!" and with this the dolls' mistress dropped Raggedy Ann on the floor and left the room.

When she came back she had on an apron and her sleeves were rolled up.

She picked up all the sticky dolls and putting them in a basket she carried them out under the apple tree in the garden.

There she had placed her little tub and wringer and she took the dolls one at a time, and scrubbed them with a scrubbing brush and soused them up and down and this way and that in the soap suds until they were clean.

Then she hung them all out on the clothes-line in the sunshine to dry.

There the dolls hung all day, swinging and twisting about as the breeze swayed the clothes-line.

"I do believe she scrubbed my face so hard she wore off my smile!" said Raggedy Ann, after an hour of silence.

"No, it is still there!" said the tin soldier, as the wind twisted him around so he could see Raggedy. "But I do believe my arms will never work without squeaking, they feel so rusted," he added.

Just then the wind twisted the little Dutch doll and loos-

ened his clothes-pin, so that he fell to the grass below with a sawdusty bump and as he rolled over he said, "Mamma!" in a squeaky voice.

Late in the afternoon the back door opened and the little mistress came out with a table and chairs. After setting the table she took all the dolls from the line and placed them about the table.

They had lemonade with grape jelly in it, which made it a beautiful lavender color, and little "Baby-teeny-weeny-cookies" with powdered sugar on them.

After this lovely dinner, the dollies were taken in the house, where they had their hair brushed and nice clean nighties put on.

Then they were placed in their beds and Mistress kissed each one good night and tiptoed from the room closing the door very gently behind her.

All the dolls lay as still as mice for a few minutes, then Raggedy Ann raised upon her cotton-stuffed elbows and said: "I have been thinking!"

"Sh!" said all the other dollies, "Raggedy has been thinking!"

"Yes," said Raggedy Ann, "I have been thinking our mistress gave us the nice dinner out under the trees to teach us a lesson. She wanted to teach us that we could have had all the goodies we wished, if we had behaved ourselves. And our lesson was that we must never take without asking what we could always have for the asking! So let us all remember and try never again to do anything which might cause those who love us any unhappiness of any kind!"

"Let us all remember," chimed all the other dollies.

And Raggedy Ann, with a merry twinkle in her shoe-but-

ton eyes, lay back in her little bed, her cotton head filled with thoughts of love and happiness.

RAGGEDY ANN AND THE KITE

RAGGEDY ANN AND THE KITE

RAGGEDY Ann watched with interest the preparations. A number of sticks were being fastened together with strings and covered with light cloth.

Raggedy Ann heard some of the boys talk of "The Kite," so Raggedy Ann knew this must be a kite.

When a tail had been fastened to the kite and a large ball of heavy twine tied to the front, one of the boys walked off, unwinding the ball of twine.

There was a nice breeze blowing, so the boy with the twine called, "Let 'er go!" and started running.

Marcella held Raggedy up so that she could watch.

How nicely it climbed! But suddenly the kite acted strangely, and as all the children shouted advice to the boy with the ball of twine, the kite began darting this way and that, and finally making four or five loop-the-loops, it crashed to the ground.

"It needs more tail on it!" one boy shouted.

Then the children asked each other where they might get more rags to fasten to the tail of th kite.

"Let's tie Raggedy Ann to the tail!" suggested Marcella. "I know she would enjoy the trip way up in the sky!"

The boys all shouted with delight at this new suggestion. So Raggedy Ann was tied to the tail of the kite.

This time the kite rose straight in the air and remained steady. The ball of twine unwound until the kite and Raggedy Ann were 'way, way up and far away. How Raggedy Ann enjoyed being up there! She could see for miles and miles! And how tiny the children looked!

Suddenly a great puff of wind came and carried Raggedy Ann streaming way out behind the kite! She could hear the wind singing on the twine as the strain increased.

Suddenly Raggedy Ann felt something rip. It was the rag to which she was tied. As each puff of wind caught her the rip widened.

When Marcella watched Raggedy Ann rise high above the field, she wondered how much Raggedy Ann enjoyed it, and wished that she, too, might have gone along. But after the kite had been up in the air for five or ten minutes, Marcella grew restless. Kites were rather tiresome. There was more fun in tea parties out under the apple tree.

"Will you please pull down the kite now?" she asked the boy with the twine. "I want Raggedy Ann."

"Let her ride up there!" the boy replied. "We'll bring her home when we pull down the kite! We're going to get another ball of twine and let her go higher!"

Marcella did not like to leave Raggedy Ann with the boys, so she sat down upon the ground to wait until they pulled

down the kite.

But while Marcella watched Raggedy Ann, a dot in the sky, she could not see the wind ripping the rag to which Raggedy was tied.

Suddenly the rag parted and Raggedy Ann went sailing away as the wind caught in her skirts.

Marcella jumped from the ground, too surprised to say anything. The kite, released from the weight of Raggedy Ann began darting and swooping to the ground.

"We'll get her for you!" some of the boys said when they saw Marcella's troubled face, and they started running in the direction Raggedy Ann had fallen. Marcella and the other girls ran with them. They ran, and they ran, and they ran, and at last they found the kite upon the ground with one of the sticks broken, but they could not find Raggedy Ann anywhere.

"She must have fallen almost in your yard!" a boy said to Marcella, "for the kite was directly over here when the doll fell!"

Marcella was heartbroken. She went in the house and lay on the bed. Mamma went out with the children and tried to find Raggedy Ann, but Raggedy Ann was nowhere to be seen.

When Daddy came home in the evening he tried to find Raggedy, but met with no success. Marcella had eaten hardly any dinner, nor could she be comforted by Mamma or Daddy. The other dolls in the nursery lay forgotten and were not put to bed that night, for Marcella lay and sobbed and tossed about her bed.

Finally she said a little prayer for Raggedy Ann, and went to sleep. And as she slept Marcella dreamed that the fairies came and took Raggedy Ann with them to fairyland for a visit, and then sent Raggedy Ann home to her. She awakened with a cry. Of course Mamma came to her bed right away and said that Daddy would offer a reward in the morning for the return of Raggedy.

"It was all my fault, Mamma!" Marcella said. "I should not have offered the boys dear old Raggedy Ann to tie on the tail of a kite! But I just know the fairies will send her back."

Mamma took her in her arms and soothed her with cheering words, although she felt indeed that Raggedy Ann was truly lost and would never be found again.

Now, where do you suppose Raggedy Ann was all this time?

When Raggedy Ann dropped from the kite, the wind caught in her skirts and carried her along until she fell in the fork of the large elm tree directly over Marcella's house. When Raggedy Ann fell with a thud, face up in the fork of the tree, two robins who had a nest near by flew chattering away.

Presently the robins returned and quarreled at Raggedy Ann for lying so close to their nest, but Raggedy Ann only smiled at them and did not move.

When the robins quieted down and quit their quarreling, one of them hopped up closer to Raggedy Ann in order to investigate.

It was Mamma Robin. She called to Daddy Robin and

told him to come. "See the nice yarn! We could use it to line the nest with," she said.

So the robins hopped close to Raggedy Ann and asked if they might have some of her yarn hair to line their nests. Raggedy Ann smiled at them. So the two robins pulled and tugged at Raggedy Ann's yarn hair until they had enough to line their nest nice and soft.

Evening came and the robins sang their good night songs, and Raggedy Ann watched the stars come out, twinkle all night and disappear in the morning light. In the morning the robins again pulled yarn from Raggedy Ann's head, and loosened her so she could peep over the side of the limb, and when the sun came up Raggedy Ann saw she was in the trees in her own yard.

Now before she could eat any breakfast, Marcella started out to find Raggedy Ann. And it was Marcella herself who found her. And this is how she did it.

Mamma Robin had seen Marcella with Raggedy Ann out in the yard many times, so she began calling "Cheery! Cheery!" and Daddy Robin started calling "Cheery! Cheery! Cheer up! Cheer up! Cheerily! Cheerily! Cheery! Cheery!" And Marcella looking up into the tree above the house to see the robins, discovered Raggedy Ann peeping over the limb at her.

Oh, how her heart beat with happiness. "Here is Raggedy Ann," she shouted as she ran toward the house.

And Mamma and Daddy came out and saw Raggedy smiling at them, and Daddy got the clothes prop and climbed out of the attic window and poked Raggedy Ann out of the tree and she fell right into Marcella's arms where she was hugged in a tight embrace.

"You'll never go up on a kite again, Raggedy Ann!" said Marcella, "for I felt so lost without you. I will never let you leave me again."

So Raggedy Ann went into the house and had breakfast with her little mistress and Mamma and Daddy smiled at each other when they peeped through the door into the breakfast room, for Raggedy Ann's smile was wide and very yellow. Marcella, her heart full of happiness, was feeding Raggedy Ann part of her egg.

RAGGEDY ANN RESCUES FIDO

RAGGEDY ANN RESCUES FIDO

I T WAS almost midnight and the dolls were asleep in their beds; all except Raggedy Ann.

Raggedy lay there, her shoe-button eyes staring straight up at the ceiling. Every once in a while Raggedy Ann ran her rag hand up through her yarn hair. She was thinking.

When she had thought for a long, long time, Raggedy Ann raised herself on her wobbly elbows and said, "I've thought it all out."

At this the other dolls shook each other and raised up saying, "Listen! Raggedy has thought it all out!"

"Tell us what you have been thinking, dear Raggedy," said the tin soldier. "We hope they were pleasant thoughts."

"Not very pleasant thoughts!" said Raggedy, as she brushed a tear from her shoe-button eyes. "You haven't seen Fido all day, have you?"

"Not since early this morning," the French dolly said.

"It has troubled me," said Raggedy, "and if my head was not stuffed with lovely new white cotton, I am sure it would have ached with the worry! When Mistress took me into the living-room this afternoon she was crying, and I heard her mamma say, 'We will find him! He is sure to come home soon!' and I knew they were talking of Fido! He must be lost!"

The tin soldier jumped out of bed and ran over to Fido's basket, his tin feet clicking on the floor as he went. "He is not here," he said.

"When I was sitting in the window about noon-time," said the Indian doll, "I saw Fido and a yellow scraggly dog playing out on the lawn and they ran out through a hole in the fence!"

"That was Priscilla's dog, Peterkins!" said the French doll.

"I know poor Mistress is very sad on account of Fido," said the Dutch doll, "Because I was in the dining-room at supper-time and I heard her daddy tell her to eat her supper and he would go out and find Fido; but I had forgotten all about it until now."

"That is the trouble with all of us except Raggedy Ann!" cried the little penny doll, in a squeaky voice, "She has to think for all of us!"

"I think it would be a good plan for us to show our love for Mistress and try and find Fido!" exclaimed Raggedy.

"It is a good plan, Raggedy Ann!" cried all the dolls.

"Then let us waste no more time in talking!" said Raggedy Ann, as she jumped from bed, followed by the rest.

The nursery window was open, so the dolls helped each other up on the sill and then jumped to the soft grass below. They fell in all sorts of queer attitudes, but of course the fall

did not hurt them.

At the hole in the fence the Indian doll picked up the trail of the two dogs, and the dolls, stringing out behind, followed him until they came to Peterkins' house. Peterkins was surprised to see the strange little figures in white nighties come stringing up the path to the dog house.

Peterkins was too large to sleep in the nursery, so he had a nice cozy dog-house under the grape arbor.

"Come in," Peterkins said when he saw and recognized the dolls, so all the dollies went into Peterkins' house and sat about while Raggedy told him why they had come.

"It has worried me, too!" said Peterkins, "but I had no way of telling your mistress where Fido was, for she cannot understand dog language! For you see," Peterkins continued, "Fido and I were having the grandest romp over in the park when a great big man with a funny thing on the end of a stick came running towards us. We barked at him and Fido thought he was trying to play with us and went up too close and do you know, that wicked man caught Fido in the thing at the end of the stick and carried him to a wagon and dumped him in with a lot of other dogs!"

"*The Dog Catcher!*" cried Raggedy Ann.

"Yes!" said Peterkins, as he wiped his eyes with his paws. "It was the dog catcher! For I followed the wagon at a distance and I saw him put all the dogs into a big wire pen, so that none could get out!"

"Then you know the way there, Peterkins?" asked Raggedy Ann.

"Yes, I can find it easily," Peterkins said.

"Then show us the way!" Raggedy Ann cried, "for we must try to rescue Fido."

So Peterkins led the way up alleys and across streets, the dolls all pattering along behind him. It was a strange procession. Once a strange dog ran out at them, but Peterkins told him to mind his own business and the strange dog returned to his own yard.

At last they came to the dog catcher's place. Some of the dogs in the pen were barking at the moon and others were whining and crying.

There was Fido, all covered with mud, and his pretty red ribbon dragging on the ground. My, but he was glad to see the dolls and Peterkins! All the dogs came to the side of the pen and twisted their heads from side to side, gazing in wonder at the queer figures of the dolls.

"We will try and let you out," said Raggedy Ann.

At this all the dogs barked joyfully.

Then Raggedy Ann, the other dolls and Peterkins went to the gate.

The catch was too high for Raggedy Ann to reach, but Peterkins held Raggedy Ann in his mouth and stood up on his hind legs so that she could raise the catch.

When the catch was raised, the dogs were so anxious to get out they pushed and jumped against the gate so hard it flew open, knocking Peterkins and Raggedy Ann into the mud. Such a yapping and barking was never heard in the neighborhood as when the dogs swarmed out of the enclosure, jumping over one another and scrambling about in the mad rush out the gate.

Fido picked himself up from where he had been rolled by the large dogs and helped Raggedy Ann to her feet. He, Peterkins, and all the dolls ran after the pack of dogs, turning the corner just as the dog catcher came running out of the house in his nightgown to see what was causing the trouble.

He stopped in astonishment when he saw the string of dolls in white nighties pattering down the alley, for he could not imagine what they were.

Well, you may be sure the dolls thanked Peterkins for his kind assistance and they and Fido ran on home, for a faint light was beginning to show in the east where the sun was getting ready to come up.

When they got to their own home they found an old chair out in the yard and after a great deal of work they finally dragged it to the window and thus managed to get into the nursery again.

Fido was very grateful to Raggedy Ann and the other dolls and before he went to his basket he gave them each a lick on the cheek.

The dolls lost no time in scrambling into bed and pulling up the covers, for they were very sleepy, but just as they were dozing off, Raggedy Ann raised herself and said, "If my legs and arms were not stuffed with nice clean cotton I feel sure they would ache, but being stuffed with nice clean white cotton, they do not ache and I could not feel happier if my body were stuffed with sunshine, for I know how pleased and happy Mistress will be in the morning when she discovers Fido asleep in his own little basket, safe and sound at home."

And as the dollies by this time were all asleep, Raggedy Ann pulled the sheet up to her chin and smiled so hard she ripped two stitches out of the back of her rag head.

RAGGEDY ANN AND THE PAINTER

RAGGEDY ANN AND THE PAINTER

WHEN housecleaning time came around, Mistress' mamma decided that she would have the nursery repainted and new paper put upon the walls. That was why all the dolls happened to be laid helter-skelter upon one of the high shelves.

Mistress had been in to look at them and wished to put them to bed, but as the painters were coming again in the early morning, Mamma thought it best that their beds be piled in the closet.

When all was quiet that night, Raggedy Ann who was on the bottom of the pile of dolls spoke softly and asked the others if they would mind moving along the shelf.

"The cotton in my body is getting mashed as flat as a pancake!" said Raggedy Ann. And although the tin soldier was piled so that his foot was pressed into Raggedy's face, she still wore her customary smile.

So the dolls began moving off to one side until Raggedy Ann was free to sit up.

"Ah, that's a great deal better!" she said, stretching her arms and legs and patting her dress into shape.

"Well, I'll be glad when morning comes!" she said finally, "For I know Mistress will take us out in the yard and play with us under the trees, and we may have a party."

So the dolls sat and talked until daylight, when the painters came to work.

One of the painters, a young fellow, seeing the dolls, reached up and took Raggedy Ann down from the shelf.

"Look at this rag doll, Jim," he said to one of the other painters, "She's a daisy," and he took Raggedy Ann by the hands and danced with her while he whistled a lively tune. Raggedy Ann's heels hit the floor thumpity-thump and she enjoyed it immensely.

The other dolls sat upon the shelf and looked straight before them, for it would never do to let grown-up men know that dolls were really alive.

"Better put her back upon the shelf," said one of the other men. "You'll have the little girl after you! The chances are that she likes that old rag doll better than any of the others!"

But the young painter twisted Raggedy Ann into funny attitudes and laughed and laughed as she looped about. Finally he got to tossing her up in the air and catching her. This was great fun for Raggedy and as she sailed up by the shelf the dolls all smiled at her, for it pleased them whenever Raggedy Ann was happy.

But the young fellow threw Raggedy Ann up into the air once too often and when she came down he failed to catch

her and she came down *splash*, head first into a bucket of oily paint.

"I told you!" said the older painter, "and now you are in for it!"

"My goodness! I didn't mean to do it!" said the young fellow, "What had I better do with her?"

"Better put her back on the shelf!" replied the other.

So Raggedy was placed back upon the shelf and the paint ran from her head and trickled down upon her dress.

After breakfast, Mistress came into the nursery and saw Raggedy all covered with paint and she began crying.

The young painter felt sorry and told her how it had happened.

"If you will let me," he said, "I will take her home with me and will clean her up tonight and will bring her back day after tomorrow."

So Raggedy was wrapped in a newspaper that evening and carried away.

All the dolls felt sad that night without Raggedy Ann near them.

"Poor Raggedy! I could have cried when I saw her all covered with paint!" said the French doll.

"She didn't look like our dear old Raggedy Ann at all!" said the tin soldier, who wiped the tears from his eyes so that they would not run down on his arms and rust them.

"The paint covered her lovely smile and nose and you could not see the laughter in her shoe-button eyes!" said the Indian doll.

And so the dolls talked that night and the next. But in the daytime when the painters were there, they kept very quiet.

The second day Raggedy was brought home and the dolls were all anxious for night to come so that they could see and talk with Raggedy Ann.

At last the painters left and the house was quiet, for Mistress had been in and placed Raggedy on the shelf with the other dolls.

"Tell us all about it, Raggedy dear!" the dolls cried.

"Oh I am so glad I fell in the paint!" cried Raggedy, after she had hugged all the dolls, "For I have had the happiest time. The painter took me home and told his Mamma how I happened to be covered with paint and she was very sorry. She took a rag and wiped off my shoe-button eyes and then I saw that she was a very pretty, sweet-faced lady and she got some gasoline and wiped off most of the paint on my face.

"But you know," Raggedy continued, "the paint had soaked through my rag head and had made the cotton inside all sticky and soggy and I could not think clearly. And my yarn hair was all matted with paint.

"So the kind lady took off my yarn hair and cut the stitches out of my head and took out all the painty cotton.

"It was a great relief, although it felt queer at first and my thoughts seemed scattered.

"She left me in her work-basket that night and hung me out upon the clothes-line the next morning when she had washed the last of the paint off.

"And while I hung out on the clothes-line, what do you think?"

"We could never guess!" all the dolls cried.

"Why a dear little Jenny Wren came and picked enough cotton out of me to make a cute little cuddly nest in the grape arbor!"

"Wasn't that sweet!" cried all the dolls.

"Yes indeed it was!" replied Raggedy Ann, "It made me very happy. Then when the lady took me in the house again she stuffed me with lovely nice new cotton, all the way from my knees up and sewed me up and put new yarn on my head for hair and—and—and it's a secret!" said Raggedy Ann.

"Oh tell us the secret!" cried all the dolls, as they pressed closer to Raggedy. "Well, I know you will not tell anyone who would not be glad to know about it, so I will tell you the secret and why I am wearing my smile a trifle broader!" said Raggedy Ann.

The dolls all said that Raggedy Ann's smile was indeed a quarter of an inch wider on each side.

"When the dear lady put the new white cotton in my body," said Raggedy Ann, "she went to the cupboard and came back with a paper bag. And she took from the bag ten or fifteen little candy hearts with mottoes on them and she hunted through the candy hearts until she found a beautiful red one which she sewed up in me with the cotton! So that is the secret, and that is why I am so happy! Feel here," said Raggedy Ann. All the dolls could feel Raggedy Ann's beautiful new candy heart and they were very happy for her.

After all had hugged each other good night and had

cuddled up for the night, the tin soldier asked, "Did you have a chance to see what the motto on your new candy heart was, Raggedy Ann?"

"Oh yes," replied Raggedy Ann, "I was so happy I forgot to tell you. It had printed upon it in nice blue letters, "I LOVE YOU.""

RAGGEDY ANN'S TRIP ON THE RIVER

RAGGEDY ANN'S TRIP
ON THE RIVER

WHEN Marcella had a tea party out in the orchard, of course all of the dolls were invited. Raggedy Ann, the tin soldier, the Indian doll and all the others—even the four little penny dolls in the spool box. After a lovely tea party with ginger cookies and milk, of course the dolls were very sleepy, at least Marcella thought so, so she took all except Raggedy Ann into the house and put them to bed for the afternoon nap. Then Marcella told Raggedy Ann to stay there and watch the things.

As there was nothing else to do, Raggedy Ann waited for Marcella to return. And as she watched the little ants eating cookie crumbs Marcella had thrown to them, she heard all of a sudden the patter of puppy feet behind her. It was Fido.

The puppy dog ran up to Raggedy Ann and twisted his head about as he looked at her. Then he put his front feet out and barked in Raggedy Ann's face. Raggedy Ann tried to look very stern, but she could not hide the broad smile painted on her face.

"Oh, you want to play, do you?" the puppy barked, as he jumped at Raggedy Ann and then jumped back again.

The more Raggedy Ann smiled, the livelier Fido's antics became, until finally he caught the end of her dress and dragged her about.

This was great fun for the puppy dog, but Raggedy Ann did not enjoy it. She kicked and twisted as much as she could, but the puppy dog thought Raggedy Ann was playing.

He ran out the garden gate and down the path across the meadow. Every once in a while Fido would give Raggedy Ann a great shaking, making her yarn head hit the ground "ratty-tat-tat." Then he would give his head a toss and send Raggedy Ann high in the air.

By this time, she had lost her apron and now some of her yarn hair was coming loose.

As Fido neared the brook, another puppy dog came running across the foot-bridge to meet him. "What have you there, Fido?" said the new puppy dog as he bounced up to Raggedy Ann.

"This is Raggedy Ann," answered Fido. "She and I are having a lovely time playing."

You see, Fido really thought Raggedy enjoyed being tossed around and whirled high up in the air. But of course she didn't. However, the game didn't last much longer. As Raggedy Ann hit the ground the new puppy dog caught her dress and ran with her across the bridge, Fido barking close behind him.

In the center of the bridge, Fido caught up with the new puppy dog and they had a lively tug-of-war with Raggedy Ann stretched between them. As they pulled and tugged and flopped Raggedy Ann about, somehow she fell over the side of the bridge into the water.

The puppy dogs were surprised, and Fido was very sorry indeed, for he remembered how good Raggedy Ann had been to him and how she had rescued him from the dog-pound. But the current carried Raggedy Ann along and all Fido could do was to run along the bank and bark.

Now, you would have thought Raggedy Ann would sink, but no, she floated nicely, for she was stuffed with clean white cotton and the water didn't soak through very quickly.

After a while, the strange puppy and Fido grew tired of running along the bank and the strange puppy scampered home over the meadow, as if he had nothing to be ashamed of. But Fido walked home very sorry indeed. His little heart was broken to think that he had caused Raggedy Ann to be drowned.

But Raggedy Ann didn't drown—not a bit of it. In fact, she even went to sleep on the brook, for the motion of the current was very soothing as it carried her along—just like being rocked by Marcella.

So, sleeping peacefully, Raggedy Ann drifted along until she lodged against a large stone.

Raggedy Ann tried to climb upon the stone, but by this time the water had thoroughly soaked through Raggedy Ann's nice, clean, white cotton stuffing and she was so heavy she could not climb.

So there she had to stay until Marcella and Daddy came

along and found her.

You see, they had been looking for her. They had found pieces of her apron all along the path where Fido and the strange puppy dog had shaken them from Raggedy Ann. So they followed the brook until they found her.

When Daddy fished Raggedy Ann from the water, Marcella hugged her so tightly to her breast the water ran from Raggedy Ann and dripped all over Marcella's apron. But Marcella was so glad to find Raggedy Ann again she didn't mind it a bit. She just hurried home and took off all of Raggedy Ann's wet clothes and placed her on a little red chair in front of the oven door, and then brought all of the other dolls in and read a fairy tale to them while Raggedy Ann steamed and dried.

When Raggedy Ann was thoroughly dry, Mamma said

she thought the cake must be finished and she took from the oven a lovely chocolate cake and gave Marcella a large piece to have another tea party with.

That night when all the house was asleep, Raggedy Ann raised up in bed and said to the dolls who were still awake, "I am so happy I do not feel a bit sleepy. Do you know, I believe the water soaked me so thoroughly my candy heart must have melted and filled my whole body, and I do not feel the least bit angry with Fido for playing with me so roughly!"

So all the other dolls were happy, too, for happiness is

very easy to catch when we love one another and are sweet
all through.